Ann Turnbull was brought up in south-east London but now lives in the West Midlands. She has always loved reading, and knew from the age of ten that she wanted to be a writer. Her numerous books for children include *No Friend of Mine, Room for a Stranger, A Long Way Home* and *House of Ghosts*. Ann's popular title *Pigeon Summer* was shortlisted for the Smarties Book Prize and the WH Smith Mind-Boggling Books Award, and has also been dramatized for televi-ion by Channel 4. She says of *Deep Water*, "Jon is n a dilemma. He tells a lie and then struggles to scape its consequences. I found it fascinating to t myself in his place and imagine how he uld react as events closed in on him."

Books by the same author

*House of Ghosts*

*A Long Way Home*

*Pigeon Summer*

*No Friend of Mine*

*Room for a Stranger*

For older readers

*No Shame, No Fear*

# DEEP WATER

Ann Turnbull

WALKER BOOKS
AND SUBSIDIARIES
LONDON • BOSTON • SYDNEY • AUCKLAND

This is a work of fiction. Names, characters, places and incidents are either the product of the author's imagination or, if real, are used fictitiously.

This edition published 2004 by Walker Books Ltd
87 Vauxhall Walk, London SE11 5HJ

2 4 6 8 10 9 7 5 3 1


Cover photograph: Bluegreen Pictures
Cover design by Walker Books Ltd



This book has been typeset in ITC Highlander

Printed and bound in Great Britain by Bookmarque Ltd, Croydon, Surrey



British Library Cataloguing in Publication Data:
a catalogue record for this book
is available from the British Library

ISBN 1-84428-643-6

www.walkerbooks.co.uk

*I would like to thank Frank Watson*
*for his help with the research for this book*

# Chapter One

The bus was late. Jon hoped it had broken down. Or caught fire. Or been hijacked. Anything – so long as he didn't have to go to school this Friday.

Today, if he went in, he'd be given his report to take home. And then the trouble would start: Mum cross-examining him, nagging, bullying. He'd never hear the end of it.

"Hey, Jon!" Ryan Jackson crossed the road, grinning. "You off to that posh school?"

Jon hated being seen in his school uniform. The black blazer with its blue and gold badge marked him out as different: the only one on the

Eldon Wood estate who didn't go to the local school.

"Bus is late," he growled.

"Skive off, then," suggested Ryan. "Say it never came."

Jon considered the possibility. A day's reprieve. No, three, with the weekend. He'd thought of skipping school before. It wasn't just the lessons. It was the other boys – the gangs and the bullying; being always on the outside of things.

"I'll come with you," said Ryan. "I hate Fridays. We get old Fraser for maths. We could go over the canal. You know Gaz? Fell in last week. Nearly drowned..."

Jon laughed. Across the road he saw fields, woods, the glint of water.

If only he dared... But Mum would find out. And her anger would be terrifying.

"You could forge a note," Ryan said. "They never look at those notes."

Jon thought they would at the Thomas

Crawford School. It was the sort of school where they kept a check on you. But the bus wasn't coming. If it doesn't come, he thought, it'll be all right. I can go with Ryan. It won't be my fault.

"This uniform," he said. "I'd have to change..."

"Let's go to your house, then." Ryan walked to the kerb and stood there, grinning. "You coming? Or are you scared?"

Jon didn't want to look soft. Ryan was his only friend.

"I'm coming," he said.

They darted across the road and onto the footpath that led to the estate. Jon heard a familiar sound and looked back.

The school bus.

If he ran, now, he could be across the road and back at the stop in time. He thought of the boys who made every morning a misery on that bus: Simon Ray and Stefan Coltswood.

He followed Ryan.

* * *

He sneaked into the empty house the back way, just in case any neighbours were watching. Not that the neighbours were likely to say anything to his mum; she didn't spend much time with them. He put his school clothes away and got dressed in jeans and jumper. Catching sight of himself in the mirror he felt scared. Suppose Mum found out? What could he say? That he'd thought he must have missed the bus? Yes, that would do.

Ryan was waiting outside.

They crossed the estate and went out through an underpass that led to the canal towpath. No one was around. It was early: still only ten past eight.

"Your mum'd have a fit if she could see you," said Ryan.

Jon knew it was true. Not only because he was playing truant but because he was with Ryan. He tried to look unconcerned.

"What about yours?" he asked.

"She doesn't care."

On the canal two swans were swimming around a half-sunken supermarket trolley. They hissed and lifted their wings as the boys came near.

But Ryan wasn't interested in swans. There was a pipe across the canal, and he showed Jon how he could balance along it, arms spread, wobbling.

"This is where Gaz fell in," he said.

Jon took a turn. It was difficult. He had to climb over a fan of spikes to get onto the pipe and, once there, up and balancing on the curve, the sight of the water below made him unsteady. Ryan began drumming on the pipe, sending vibrations down its length.

"Don't!" Jon reached the spikes on the far side and clambered to safety. "Race you to the bridge!"

They arrived together, breathless, disputing who'd won. At last Jon was beginning to enjoy himself.

"Let's go underneath," he said.

The towpath was slippery, and their voices echoed.

Ryan boasted, "I saw a dead dog in here once."

"You didn't!"

"I did! You ask Jamie Kendrick. He was with me. It was all swollen up, like a balloon."

"Ugh!"

Ryan pushed him, making him stagger. "Mind you don't fall in!"

"Get off!"

They found stones and aimed them across the canal at a metal fence on the other side. The stones rang out as they hit home.

A woman came out of a cottage further up the towpath and stared, hands on hips.

They sauntered past her, but when Jon turned round, she was still watching them suspiciously.

They left the canal and walked across fields to the Summerlees estate. There was a wooded area on the far side where a rope swing hung over a ravine. They took turns to swing out over the drop, twisting and laughing. Then they found a den that someone had made near by and took it over. It was good having the place to themselves.

At eleven o'clock Jon said, "I'm starving."

They went to the fish and chip shop on the estate, bought chips and Coke and walked back eating.

Jon told Ryan about the report.

"Chuck it."

"Can't. You have to return a slip. And there's a parents' evening soon. She'd find out."

"My mum never bothers with parents' evenings," said Ryan.

He screwed up the greasy paper and dropped it over someone's hedge. "Where shall we go? Town centre?"

"No..." Jon thought his mother might be shopping there in her lunch-hour. "We could go down to the river. It said on the news there were floods."

A field path took them into woodland with drifts of bluebells. It was two miles to the river.

They met a woman walking a dog, but no one else. Ryan chatted: about his dogs, his mum's boyfriend, who'd let him have a go on his motor-bike, his mates at school – Gaz, Jamie, Sandeep, Baggsey. Jon remembered the names from junior school, but he'd lost touch with most of them; only Ryan had stayed friends with him.

They came out on the riverbank.

The river was high, lapping at the footpath which ran alongside back garden gates and fences.

"It's under water further up," said Ryan.

He led the way.

Jon threw a stick into the water and watched the current snatch it. If you fell in, he thought, you'd be done for.

"Jon! Look at this!"

Ryan, ahead of him, was parting a clump of nettles.

Jon ran to see.

It was a boat: a small rowing boat, upturned, abandoned.

# Chapter Two

"We could get it afloat!" Ryan said. "There's nothing wrong with it. Give us a hand, Jon – turn it over. Come on!"

Jon hesitated. The boat must belong to someone. He glanced at the nearest house. It was separated from the river by a long garden, overgrown with weeds. The gate looked as if it hadn't been opened for years.

"No one lives there," said Ryan.

"They might. You can't see."

"They've dumped it, though, haven't they? Must have."

"I don't know."

"It's not stealing," Ryan argued. "Not if it's on the bank. It would be if it was in the garden."

Jon supposed he was right. And the boat did look as if it had been abandoned. He waded in among the nettles and examined it more closely. It was dark, its surface covered with slimy green algae.

Ryan banged on the planking. "It'll float. Come on, let's try it."

He heaved at one side. Jon went to help him. The boat was surprisingly heavy, but between them they lifted it, revealing whitened grass beneath. They rolled it over onto its bottom.

"Hey! A paddle!" said Ryan, and grabbed it.

There were two plank seats.

Ryan tried to push the boat towards the water. "Come on!"

Jon felt uneasy. It seemed wrong. He looked around at the back gardens and the riverbank. No one was there. No anglers. No one walking a dog. He found himself wishing someone *would* see them; someone who'd call out, chase them off...

"Grab the other end," said Ryan.

They half carried, half dragged the boat down to the water. The river was so high that they soon felt it taking the weight from their arms. No water seeped between the planks.

"Get in," said Ryan. "I'll hold it steady."

Cautiously Jon climbed in. The boat rocked, and he staggered and sat down. Ryan was struggling to hold on against the pull of the river.

"Quick!" said Jon – afraid of being launched in the boat alone.

Ryan climbed in. He picked up the paddle and pushed off from the bank. The boat floated out into the middle of the river, rocking on the current. It felt peaceful. Jon relaxed and gazed over the side. The water was yellow-brown; thick coils of weed swayed below its surface.

"I'll take us to the other bank," said Ryan.

He struggled with the paddle at first, but soon the boat began to move in the direction he wanted. He laughed. "This is great!" He flicked water at Jon, and Jon ducked, making the boat dip. "Watch out!" Laughing, they wrestled for control of the paddle.

The boat touched against the bank on the far side. Jon looked back and saw that they had not travelled in a straight line. The current had carried them downstream.

Ryan turned the prow and began paddling back towards their starting place, but the current was too strong for him and they drifted on. There were no more houses here, and no footpath. A tangle of half-submerged trees and bushes stood up out of the water. As Ryan tried to reach the shore the boat was caught among them.

"We can't land here."

"We'll have to go back."

Jon took the paddle and battled with the current. It was no good. They were still drifting downstream.

"Where does it go – the river?" he asked.

"Don't know."

Jon felt that they were heading towards the town. Perhaps they could float home. There must be somewhere else they could land. He grew tired and Ryan took the paddle.

Jon watched the broad brown sweep of the river ahead, the drowned trees and broken branches caught in the flood.

The current pulled at the boat. It was getting stronger. The banks slid by faster and faster, and the water was choppy. Jon noticed small eddies and whirlpools. He felt a flicker of anxiety.

"Try and land," he said. "Over there. See that tree lying in the water? We might be able to climb along the trunk to the shore."

Ryan attempted to turn the boat, but the current pulled him off-course, and he missed the place Jon had seen. A small whirlpool caught them, turning them slowly, helplessly. For a moment they found themselves facing upstream and drifting backwards. Jon began to feel afraid;

they had no control. They were like that twig he'd dropped into the water.

"We must stop," he said. "We must."

They were closer to the shore now, but the banks had become wooded cliffs rising straight up out of the water, with rocks around their base. Jon noticed white water ahead. Cross-currents tugged at the boat, half-turning it, then letting it go.

"It's getting rough," Ryan said.

Jon noticed the fear in his friend's voice, and that scared him; Ryan was never afraid.

Just ahead of them now he saw the undulating brown surface of the river broken by white foam. Suddenly he understood: rocks! He saw the black deadly tip of one breaking the surface.

"Ryan!" he yelled. "Rocks! Rocks up ahead! Turn away, quick!"

Ryan thrust with the paddle. The boat swung out just in time to miss the rock. Jon could have touched it with his hand as they swept by. But there were more rocks ahead – more and more flurries of white foam. And they were being driven towards them, towards the shore.

"Help!" they shouted. "Help!" But there was no one to hear.

The paddle snapped against a rock. The jolt almost pulled Ryan overboard. He tossed the broken end into the water.

"We're going to crash!"

Jon heard a bang, felt the shock of the impact shudder through his bones, heard wood splinter and saw Ryan flung towards the rocks. And then there was water, ice-cold, deadly, pulling him down and closing over his head.

# Chapter Three

He began fighting his way up through the water. His chest felt as if it would burst, and the cold seemed to penetrate his bones.

He broke the surface, scraping his arm on a rock. That rock was his chance: he grabbed it and clung on. The river fought him, dragging him back. His hands slipped. In desperation he forced his lower body out of the water and felt the river relinquish its grip. He was safe. He crawled from rock to rock until he reached the shore and lay there, trembling with exhaustion.

Ryan...?

Ryan was a few metres away, lying face down

on the rocks, clear of the water.

Jon got up and staggered towards him.

"Ryan? You all right?"

Ryan lifted his head and whispered, "Hurts..." His face was white with pain. Jon felt scared.

"What hurts?" His hand hovered nervously near Ryan's shoulder. He didn't know what to do.

"Arm ... across here ... everything."

"Can you get up?"

Ryan drew his knees up and tried to get onto all fours. But when he moved his left arm he cried out in pain.

"Is it broken?"

"I think so."

Jon took hold of the other arm and helped him to his feet. Ryan moved about cautiously, wincing. Jon remembered seeing him flung onto the rocks; he must be covered in bruises – but at least he was dry.

"You're soaked," said Ryan.

Jon nodded, shivering. He squeezed out his

wet clothes and took his trainers off and emptied them. It ought to have been funny – like Gaz falling in the canal – but neither of them laughed.

Jon looked out across the river. The boat had sunk; the broken paddle had been swept away. And behind them – the only way out – was a steep cliff.

"We could climb it," said Ryan.

"With that arm?"

"You'd have to help me. We can't stay here, can we?"

"You need a sling." Jon was excited, remembering something. He took off his T-shirt, put the neck opening over Ryan's head and made the rest of it into a bag to support the injured arm.

Ryan grinned. "That's ace."

"My dad showed me," said Jon.

"You still see him then?"

"Sometimes." Jon put his jumper back on. "You go first. Then if you slip, I'll be behind you."

The cliff was high, but the part they could see, at the bottom, didn't look too difficult to climb. Higher up there were more trees and bushes growing out of it, and the top was hidden by the leaves.

Ryan began climbing one-handed. It was easy at first; there were big outcrops of rock, and plenty of footholds and handholds, and Ryan was a good climber. The arm hurt him; several times he stopped and gasped in pain. But when Jon asked if he wanted to come down he said, "No way. I'm going up. Got to get out of here."

Jon saw a ledge a little way above them. Ryan was intent on reaching it. The cliff rose steeply, and there were no easy handholds. Jon, coming up behind, saw Ryan struggling to hold on to the trunk of a small tree and swing himself up.

"I can't do it!" Ryan exclaimed in sudden pain and panic. "Jon, give us a bunk up."

Jon pushed from behind and Ryan, gasping with pain, scrambled onto the ledge and crouched there, shaking.

Jon landed beside him. He realized now that Ryan couldn't go on. Above them the cliff was smooth and steep with only the trees to hold on to, and the top curved outwards in an overhang.

"Could you get down again?" Jon asked.

Ryan looked back the way they had come and shook his head.

"Try?"

"No." All the enterprise had gone from Ryan; his face was pinched with pain. "You'll have to go up. Get help. I'm staying here."

"Will you be all right?"

Ryan nodded, clenching his teeth.

"I'll be quick," said Jon. "Don't worry."

Ryan managed a grin. "Hey – do you think I'll get to go in an ambulance? I've never been in one before."

Jon reached for the trunk of a young tree and swung himself up.

It wasn't difficult to climb using bushes and

small footholds, but it was frightening. Jon fought down his fear and moved fast, conscious of Ryan's eyes on him, and feeling that Ryan would have done it easily if he'd had both hands. It was only when he reached the overhang that he faltered. He found himself leaning back over the drop, trusting to the bushes to hold his weight. Just below the summit he hung, shaking with cold, terrified. But there was no one to help him, and at last he hauled himself up, grabbed for a tree root, and with an enormous effort managed to scramble over the top.

Cautiously, on hands and knees, he turned round.

From here he couldn't see Ryan. He couldn't see the shore at all, just descending layers of leaves and beneath them the river and the rocks breaking its surface. He shouted, "Ryan! Can you hear me? I've made it! I won't be long!"

He heard a faint shout in reply.

A few metres in from the cliff edge was a

metal barrier. He climbed over it on to a road. It was a narrow country road with no pavement, bordered by woods on either side. He looked back, fixing the place in his memory: two silver birches close to the barrier. He ought to make a sign, he thought. He took off one of his socks and hung it in a cleft in the nearest birch. Then he turned towards the road, brushing dirt from his clothes.

Which way should he go? He had no idea where he was. To his right the road was straight, empty. To the left there was a bend. He began walking left.

A car passed him, going fast. Jon thought, I should have flagged it down, asked for help. The next one that comes...

He turned the bend in the road and saw another endless stretch. No houses, no telephone box. He walked on. On the opposite side of the road a track led into the woods. There was a footpath sign. He crossed over to read it:

**Eldon Wood 2. Summerlees 2 ½**

Eldon Wood. Home. He wasn't far from home after all. He visualized the telephone on the hall table; he could phone from there. Of course it might be quicker to flag down a driver. But the road was empty, and he didn't know how soon someone would come. It would be better to go home. He turned onto the track and began to run.

By the time he reached the estate his clothes were almost dry, and no one seemed to take any notice of him as he ran through. At half past four he was home. He went to the shed in the back garden and found the spare key and opened the front door. There, on the hall table, was the telephone.

Jon became aware that he was shaking with cold. He struggled with stiff fingers to undo the laces of his trainers. The shoes were waterlogged.

He pulled them off and walked across the carpet in his wet sock to the hall table.

There was a mirror above it. He was shocked by his appearance: mauve skin, stringy hair, the red mark of a graze on the inside of his left arm. And there was dirt all down the front of his jumper where he had dragged himself up the cliff.

He thought, Mum won't be home till six. I'll have time to clean myself up first; then she needn't know.

But that was stupid. He'd have to tell her what had happened.

He looked at the telephone.

He'd have to tell.

# Chapter Four

I'll phone 999, he thought. Get an ambulance – maybe a helicopter.

His hand hovered over the phone. He'd always wanted to phone 999 – now he had the chance.

Ryan would be rescued. And then – then they'd want to know how he got there and who made the phone call.

Jon thought of the stolen boat smashed on the rocks. He'd never done anything like that before. Mum would go mad.

He was scared. Scared of admitting what they had done; scared the police would be told about the missing boat; scared of Mum.

It wasn't that she hit him, or hurt him in any way; but she shouted, and he hated her shouting – he'd do anything to avoid starting her off. But worse than the anger would be her shock and disappointment. He dreaded that.

He stared at the phone.

I'll get changed, he decided. Then I'll phone.

He ran a bath. His clothes were filthy. She'd be bound to ask what he'd been doing. He bundled them up and hid them at the bottom of the laundry basket, under all the washing.

He got into the warm water and at last, gradually, he stopped shaking. The graze on his arm smarted, but he welcomed the pain; it meant the shock was wearing off.

He cleaned the bath carefully, wiping away the grimy ring. Then he dressed in clean clothes, pushed his wet trainers under the bed, and went downstairs. He got out his school-books and spread them around on the dining-room table for Mum to see. He poured himself a drink of orange and ate the last two biscuits in the tin. It was beginning to feel like a normal Friday.

Except that the phone was waiting.

I'll just ring and report the accident, he thought. Describe the place: the tree with the marker in it. They don't need to know who I am.

He lifted the receiver.

They had a way, didn't they, of tracing phone calls? He'd seen it on TV, in police dramas.

He'd give someone else's name. Gaz. "This is Gary Whittaker..." No – a made-up name. Except he couldn't think of one.

A tinny voice was speaking to him, "Please replace the handset and try again. Please replace the handset–"

He put it down.

You've got to do it, he told himself. Ryan needs help.

He picked up the receiver again and listened to its purring. He pressed 9 – then put the receiver down.

He looked at his watch. Five forty-five. Mum would be home any time.

He went into the living-room and switched on the television. Zany laughter washed over him. He paced around the room.

He thought of explaining to Mum how he'd skived off school, and with Ryan of all people, and taken the boat. He imagined her, furious, on the brink of tears, shouting about how ungrateful he was, how she struggled to pay for the uniform and the bus-fares to that school...

Someone else would find Ryan. He laughed aloud as the realization hit him. Of course. Ryan would shout. He wasn't far from the road. Someone would hear him and fetch help. He'd probably been rescued already – not even knowing that Jon hadn't phoned. And Ryan wouldn't split on him. Ryan knew what Jon's mum was like; he wouldn't drop his friend in it. Mum needn't ever know.

Mum's key turned in the lock. Jon darted to

turn off the television. Too late.

She edged in, a bulging carrier bag in either hand. "Jonathan? Are you watching TV?"

"I only just switched it on. I've done my homework."

"What was it?"

He thought of the last thing he'd done. "Writing about the Romans." He followed her into the kitchen and began unpacking, hoping she'd forget the homework. "Did you get crisps?"

"Yes. I thought you did that yesterday – the Romans."

"I wrote it out again neatly." He knew that would gain her approval.

"You'd better let me see it. Didn't you have anything else?"

"No. Well – we've got to revise. For end of term exams." At least that was true.

He watched her putting the shopping away – brisk, efficient, in her bright blue travel agency uniform. She was always busy.

She folded the empty carrier bags and put them in the cupboard. "I'm dying for a cup of tea."

"I'll make it."

She looked at him, then, sharply. "That would be nice. And we'll go over your essay."

As he reached for the kettle she said, "What have you done to your arm?"

"Oh. I – fell. At break."

"Did someone push you?"

"No. It was an accident."

"Are you sure you haven't been in a fight?"

"Yes. Why?"

But he knew why. He was nervous, and she could tell. She'd ferret it all out of him if he wasn't careful.

He poured the tea, took it into the dining-room, and found the homework.

"You haven't rewritten this."

"I have," he lied.

"You've crossed out 'army'. It was crossed out

when you showed me this yesterday."

"I – accidentally copied it the same."

"Well, write that page again neatly. And leave wider margins and put the heading in capitals."

"Oh, Mum!" he protested.

"It's scruffy, Jonathan."

"They don't mind crossings-out."

"I don't care what they mind. Anyone can do something that's good enough. I want you to do your best – so you don't end up like all the others on this estate."

Jon turned away. He didn't want to think about school. He wasn't coping, and Mr Hammond had warned him that he would probably have to be moved to a lower class next term. He hadn't dared tell Mum.

"Write it now," Mum said, "while I get changed and do the dinner."

She finished her tea and went upstairs.

"Jonathan? Have you had a bath?"

Jon thought of the wet clothes, stuffed well

down in the basket. His heart pounded. "Yes."

"I wish you'd remember to open the window. Let the steam out."

"Sorry." Relief flooded through him.

But he was shaking again, remembering the crash, the icy water, the terror as he felt he was going to drown, his arm scraping against the rocks...

"Jonathan? Are you all right?'

Mum, in jeans and a cream jumper, was back, watching him with a puzzled frown.

"You'd better get on," she said. "I'll put the pizzas in the oven. And after dinner we'll have a look at your maths. You want to do well in the exams, don't you?"

Jon couldn't finish his pizza. Over and over in his mind he relived the moment when the boat hit the rocks and he went down into the water.

Mum put her hand on his forehead. "I hope you're not sickening for something."

"I'm just tired."

"I don't know why you should be tired." Mum never let tiredness slow her down. She cleared away the dishes. As she passed the window she said, "There's Tanya – off out."

Jon jumped. Tanya was Ryan's mother. He heard Steve's motorbike revving up, and caught a glimpse, through the net curtain, of Tanya in a silver helmet, climbing on behind him.

"The size of her – and wearing those tight jeans," said Mum. "I wonder if she's got a baby-sitter. I bet they've left Ryan in charge."

"They have Nicola—" said Jon, and stopped.

"How do you know?" She narrowed her eyes. "You're not still going round there?"

"No!"

She gave him her soul-searching look. "I hope I can trust you, Jonathan."

Jon said, "I've seen her – Nicola Smith – going in."

Mum shrugged. "Well, Tanya often nips out and leaves them. I know she does."

Jon couldn't concentrate on his maths. Had Ryan been found? Surely he must have been. Tanya and Steve were on their way to the hospital – that was it.

Mum snapped the book shut. "We're not doing this for my benefit, you know. If you can't–"

The telephone interrupted her. She went out to the hall.

It was Dad; Jon could tell from her tone of voice. After the greetings there was silence on her part, then, "Well ... I don't know whether... We might be going to Jackie's..."

He's asking if I can visit, Jon thought. She always made excuses.

He hovered in the doorway.

"He's here." Mum handed over the receiver and Dad's voice, warm and uncritical, came to him. "Hi, Jon. How's it going?"

"OK."

"You don't sound OK. What's up?"

"Nothing." If Dad had been there, in person, he would have told him. But not now, over the phone. "I'm fine."

Dad began talking about a trip. "We're going to Barmouth at Whitsun." "We" meant Dad and Karen, his girlfriend. "Got a caravan. Do you want to come?"

Jon did – even though he felt strange with Karen. But he knew Mum didn't want him to go. He glanced at the open living-room door. "I might not be able to."

Dad talked about persuading Mum. Jon would enjoy it, he said, and Karen would like him to come.

"I'll ask Mum," said Jon.

But he didn't. He couldn't cope with that now. He went to bed.

Alone at last, he lay in bed but couldn't sleep. Again and again he felt the boat break up beneath him and saw Ryan flung out onto the rocks; again and again he went down into the water and struggled upwards, fighting for breath.

He was still awake when the motorbike returned and stopped outside the Jacksons' house. He heard voices, the front door shutting; then, a bit later, what sounded like an argument outside – Tanya exclaiming, Steve remonstrating. It went on for several minutes and then the door slammed and there was silence.

Jon remembered Ryan's face, white with pain, looking up at him as he climbed the cliff. He couldn't still be there. He couldn't be.

# Chapter Five

"There you are. I thought you'd never wake up."

Jon stood squinting on the landing, still half asleep.

Mum was cleaning windows. She buffed the glass, glancing into the street. "They're all out there, nattering. I had Tanya Jackson on my doorstep this morning. Seven o'clock, she came! Apparently Ryan's disappeared."

Jon was immediately wide awake. "Ryan..."

"Oh, he'll turn up. I told her, 'Don't worry.' She wanted to know if he'd stayed here. Didn't miss him till they got home last night at eleven o'clock." She shook her head; sighed. "Imagine going out, not knowing where your child is. Anyway, she's panicking now; called the police."

"The police..." Jon hoped his feelings didn't show in his face. His heart was beating so loudly he felt she must hear it.

"They'll soon find him. He'll be at someone's house. Although I wouldn't put it past Ryan to take off to London or somewhere. He's that type." She pulled the net curtain back in place and turned towards the stairs. "You'd better get some breakfast or it'll be time for lunch. There's one thing–" she laughed shortly, "the police'll know Ryan."

She *would* bring that up, Jon thought. Ryan and some others from Eldon Wood School had been caught shoplifting a year ago. That was when Mum had finally forbidden Jon from seeing Ryan. But Ryan hadn't been in trouble since.

"Ryan's all right," he said.

"I don't want you having anything to do with him. They're useless, that family."

Jon tried to eat some cornflakes. He wasn't hungry. "He might have had an accident," he said.

"If he has, it'll be because he was somewhere he shouldn't be."

That was too close to the truth. Jon fell silent.

Mum washed up and got out the vacuum cleaner. Jon scuttled upstairs to his room. He had just reached it when the front doorbell chimed.

He knew it would be the police, even before Mum opened the door.

As the uniformed policeman came in, and Mum showed him into the living-room, Jon stood stricken at the top of the stairs. If only he'd phoned yesterday. It was too late now. What could he say?

"Jonathan!" Mum called him down.

The policeman looked friendly, encouraging. But then he didn't know.

"Don't look so scared, Jonathan," he said. "Sit down. I'm PC Norris. We're making enquiries about a missing boy – Ryan Jackson. Ryan's a friend of yours, I believe?"

Jon looked at his mother. "No." His voice was husky.

"He's not?" PC Norris was clearly surprised. "Miss Jackson seems to think he is."

"Jonathan doesn't have anything to do with Ryan these days," said Mum.

"But you're neighbours, Jonathan. You do see Ryan, don't you?"

Jon avoided the policeman's eye. They know, he thought. They know I'm in on this.

"Apparently Ryan didn't turn up at school yesterday," said PC Norris.

Jon shrugged.

"Jonathan goes to the Thomas Crawford School at Overton," said Mum, and Jon heard, and hated, the pride in her voice. "He was there all day."

"What time do you leave for school, Jonathan?"

"Just before eight. The bus goes at five past eight."

"From?"

"The perimeter road. Draycott Way."

"So you walk down here, past Ryan's house, through the underpass... You must meet quite a lot of children you know."

"I'm out earlier than most of them."

"Did you see Ryan?"

"No." Jon wondered if you could be prosecuted for telling lies to the police.

"Miss Jackson says Ryan left home at eight o'clock. But you didn't see him?"

"No."

"You don't know of any reason he may have gone missing? Anyone he might be with? Any friends?"

"Jonathan doesn't mix with the local boys," Mum said.

"Gaz," said Jon. "Gary Whittaker. And David Baggs. They're his friends."

PC Norris wrote the names down and closed his notebook. "Thank you, Jonathan; Mrs Edey. Let us know if either of you remember anything. Anything at all. The smallest detail could be important."

He was gone. Jon, watching as Mum said goodbye at the door, saw that it had begun to rain.

Ryan would get wet. And it must have been cold last night. He tried to imagine being trapped on that ledge all night, and couldn't. He didn't want to imagine it. Surely Ryan couldn't still be there? And yet – if he'd been rescued, the police would have known straightaway.

Mum peeped out of the living-room window. "He's gone to the Smiths'."

Jon escaped upstairs.

From the landing window he could see a police car parked on the road. Despite the rain, people were standing about in groups, talking.

Why hadn't he told that policeman where

Ryan was? If only Mum hadn't been there. He couldn't think straight when she was around.

He watched the rain darkening the pavement. People retreated indoors. He visualized the road he had climbed on to from the cliff. A country road. No one would be walking along it now, in the pouring rain. No one would hear if Ryan shouted.

He felt suddenly angry with Ryan. It was all Ryan's fault. *He'd* suggested playing truant; *he'd* insisted on taking that boat.

It's not my fault, he told himself. I tried to help. I tried.

# Chapter Six

"I'm going to the hairdresser's this afternoon," Mum said. "I'll be a while – I'm having highlights. Now I don't want you hanging around the estate. You've got plenty of revision to do—"

"I'm going swimming with Liam and Heidi. I promised."

"All right." The Masons were one of the few families in Eldon Wood that Mum tolerated.

"But when you get back, you must do some work. Is that clear?"

"Yes. Can I have my pocket money?"

She counted out the coins. "That policeman's still up and down the street. They can't have found him yet. I'd better be going. Make sure you take one of the old towels."

"OK. Bye."

She went out. He heard the garage door opening and then the car starting up.

He ran upstairs. His window was at the back, overlooking the fields and canal. He opened it and leaned out. The rain had eased but grey clouds hid the sun and the air was cool. Stupid lot, the police. Why hadn't they found Ryan? He was only two miles away. Surely they must have been to the river? They always searched rivers when people went missing, didn't they? He thought of Ryan on that ledge, surrounded by trees. He'd climb down; he'd do it, somehow. And then someone would see him – an angler or a canoeist.

Comforted, Jon rolled up his swimming trunks in a towel and went down the road to the Masons'.

Heidi opened the door. She said, "Golda's had puppies. Come and see."

Usually Jon didn't have much time for

nine-year-old Heidi, but now he was glad to forget about Ryan and the police and look at the four Labrador puppies tumbling over each other in Golda's basket.

Heidi picked one up and let it lick her face. "This is Sandy. We're keeping her. But the others need homes. You can have one if you like."

"Mum doesn't like dogs." But he wanted a puppy. He chose one – the darkest, with big clumsy paws. Its warm tongue acknowledged him as he picked it up; its ears were silky.

"That one's a boy," said Liam.

"I like him."

"Ask your mum."

"She always says no."

Dad liked dogs. He thought of the caravan at Barmouth. Perhaps the puppy could come too?

"We'll keep him for you," said Liam, "till you ask her."

Outside, they saw a police car parked up the road.

"We've had the police round!" said Heidi.

"So have we." Jon didn't want to talk about that.

But Liam was full of speculation. "Scott Willis saw Ryan just after eight o'clock." He turned to Jon with big eyes. "He might have been the last person to see him alive."

"He's not dead!" The thought made Jon's heart race.

"Well, he might be. He might have been murdered. He might have gone off with someone. Hey, Jon – you've gone white! Just kidding. But he never turned up at school."

Jon was glad when they were in the water. For an hour he was able to stop thinking about Ryan.

On the way home, there was no sign of the police car.

They've found him, Jon thought.

He waved goodbye to Liam and turned towards his own home.

PC Norris was standing on the doorstep.

"Hello, Jonathan. Your mother doesn't seem to be in."

"She's gone to the hairdresser's." Jon's mouth felt dry.

"Perhaps I could have a quick word with you, then."

"OK." Jon scuffed one trainer on the edge of the doorstep.

"Just to clear things up. You told me you hadn't seen Ryan Jackson on Friday morning – but several people have said they saw you talking to him at the bus-stop."

"What people?" Jon felt anger surging up and was startled by it. "It wasn't me!"

"They were all sure it *was* you. They recognized your school uniform."

That uniform! He hated it. And the people – who were they? Had they seen him go off with Ryan?

"I never saw Ryan," he insisted.

"How long were you at the bus-stop?"

"Five minutes. Maybe more. The bus was late."

"But you didn't talk to anyone? No one else came to the bus-stop?"

Jon saw a way out. "It might have been Jason."

"Jason?"

"This boy I know. He said hello, stopped for a minute. It might have been him they saw. He looks a bit like Ryan."

"What's his other name? This Jason?"

"I don't know."

"Do you know where he lives?"

Jon considered the imaginary Jason. "Over Summerlees, I think."

"So you spoke to Jason at the bus-stop – for how long?"

"A couple of minutes."

"What did you talk about?"

Jon shrugged. "You know – computers and that."

"And you didn't see Ryan Jackson?"

"No."

"When did the bus come?"

"About quarter past."

"Was Jason still there when it came?'

"No. He went off."

"And you caught the bus?"

Jon's heart was fluttering. Did they know? Was this a trap?

"You got on the bus and went to school?"

They must know. They must.

He nodded, tense.

"Did you?"

Jon felt as if he were being boxed into a corner. He had to get the man's attention away from that bus-stop. He said, "I've just remembered something."

"Yes?"

"I *did* see Ryan. I was looking out of the bus window as it went round the perimeter road – near Leeson Drive – and I saw him there. He was talking to a man in a car."

PC Norris was instantly alert.

"Jonathan, you must realize this could be vital information. Why didn't you tell me before?"

"I only just remembered. It didn't seem important – I mean, people in cars often ask the way. I forgot."

He was thinking, with relief, that they couldn't have known after all that he wasn't on the bus.

"You're sure this was yesterday?"

"Yes."

"It couldn't have been the day before?"

"No."

"And are you absolutely sure it was Ryan you saw? Could it have been Jason? You said they were alike."

"No. Jason couldn't have got there that soon. And anyway, I know Ryan, he's – anyway, he was dressed different."

"Ah. What was Ryan wearing?"

Jon was confident now. "A yellow T-shirt and jeans."

"And the car? Could you describe it?"

"Red. A red Peugeot."

"And did you see the driver?"

"Not really. I mean, I was past in a minute. But he had dark hair. And I could see a blue shirtsleeve – or jacket. He was leaning out. And there was paper – like he was holding a map. Ryan was talking to him."

The scene was as vivid in Jon's mind as if he had really witnessed it. He half believed he had.

PC Norris wrote it all down. "We'll need a statement, Jonathan. Would you be prepared to come to the station later with your mother and sign a statement?"

His mother. Too late he realized he couldn't keep this secret from her. "OK," he said.

"Good. There's nothing else you can tell me now? You didn't catch a glimpse of the number plates?"

Jon shook his head. He felt dazed. What had he done? Why had he told all those lies? Everything was getting so complicated.

# *Chapter Seven*

Jon and his mother watched *The Six O'Clock News* on the television while they ate their dinner.

Ryan wasn't on the national news. But when *Midlands Today* came on, there it was: the last school photograph of Ryan. It was strange, seeing that familiar face on the screen; stranger still hearing his own lie about the man in the car turned into a news story. Police were seeking witnesses ... a red car, a Peugeot ... a dark-haired man in his thirties ... would he come forward in order to be eliminated from police enquiries. Jon began to believe it was true.

"They were quick," said Mum, "getting that on the news." It was only an hour or two since they'd come back from the police station and Jon had found himself trapped into signing a statement confirming a pack of lies. Could they get you for that, he wondered? Or was he too young? Perhaps they'd never find out. But of course they would. Ryan would tell them. Unless...

Ryan couldn't die.

"Mum," he said, "how long does it take to starve to death?"

"What? Oh, weeks, I think. Why?"

"I just wondered."

"It's water you need more than food," said Mum. "You can't live long without water."

Jon listened to the rain pattering on the window. Ryan would be all right for water. But he'd be cold. And there was no shelter – except the trees. Surely he'd be found soon – before it was dark.

The phone rang.

Jon jumped. The police! They were on to him.

Mum answered it. "Oh, hello, Jackie."

Aunty Jackie was Mum's sister. Mum settled in on the hall chair. "Yes, just highlights, but it really lifts it... Fine – and much cheaper than Crowning Glory... Oh, you don't want that, Jackie; go for the natural look ... you don't want to change the colour..."

Jon climbed the stairs. He was opening the door of his room when he heard Mum say, "Anyway, you'll never guess where else I've been today: the police station."

He went in, leaving the door ajar. Mum proceeded to give Jackie a detailed account of what Jon had told the police. It sounded more than ever to Jon as if it must really have happened, as if the dark-haired man in the red Peugeot really existed.

But if he did, he was nothing to do with Ryan's disappearance. Jon crossed to the window and watched the rainy evening darkening early and imagined people – a couple, middle-aged, with a dog – walking along that road and hearing Ryan's cries for help. He created the scene in his mind as clearly as he had created the image of the man in the red car. He willed it to happen.

Mum's tone of voice had changed. "Well, that's what I think, Jackie. I mean, you don't go out for the evening without checking whether your son's come home from school. But she never bothers. She's got this new boyfriend and a new baby, and that takes up all her attention; the others are left to their own devices..."

It's not true, Jon thought angrily. How could she say those awful things about Tanya? Tanya didn't neglect Paula and Lynette, or Ryan. It was true she didn't fuss, but that was what he liked about the Jacksons' home. Nobody bothered. Nobody nagged Ryan to do his homework or made sure he went to school. You could go round there and watch TV and drink Coke and play with the dogs, and nobody fussed or criticized.

Mum had no idea how often Jon did go round there. He was supposed to come in from school and start on his homework straight away. But she didn't get home till six; she couldn't check on him.

"...all sponging off the taxpayer," came Mum's voice now. "Two great dogs that run around the estate, messing. And four children, all by different fathers..."

Shut up, thought Jon. Leave her alone. She's my friend, and so is Ryan.

Tanya had said that, he remembered. Tanya had been on their doorstep at 7 a.m.; she'd told the police that Jon was Ryan's friend.

Some friend I've been, thought Jon.

In his imagination he ran downstairs, shouted at Mum to get off the line and call an ambulance; told her it was his fault that Ryan was missing, not Tanya's; admitted everything.

But he didn't move. It was too late. He'd told

too many lies. He didn't know how to begin to confess.

"...well, you wouldn't last long in this weather, wet through," Mum was saying. "They get hypothermia, don't they? Did you see that lad on *999*?"

Hypothermia. Wasn't that what old ladies got, freezing to death because they couldn't afford to have the heating on? Surely Ryan couldn't get that.

Mum put the phone down at last.

Jon approached her. "Could Ryan get hypothermia?"

She looked up sharply. "I wish you wouldn't listen in."

"I just heard. Can you ... die of it?"

"Of course you can. I mean, if he was outside somewhere... Of course if he went off with that man – well, I don't like to think about that."

"I'm sure he didn't. The man only seemed to be asking the way."

"I hope so. But then, where is he? It's so cold at night, and all this rain... And he might be injured."

"If he *was* injured – suppose he'd broken his arm or something – and he was stuck somewhere, but there were trees and stuff around, a bit of shelter, do you think he'd still be all right?"

Mum stared at him, and he felt himself going red.

"You're not hiding anything, are you, Jonathan? *Did* you speak to Ryan? Do you know where he is?"

Jon opened his mouth; drew breath. He was on the brink of confession. It would be such a relief to drop the load of guilt. But Mum went on, "If you're in on this, Jonathan, if you've let me down, I'll never be able to hold my head up around here again. *Do* you know where Ryan is?" Her eyes were pleading. He realized that she was afraid he was involved and desperate to be reassured that he wasn't. He told her what she wanted to hear.

"No," he said. "No. I never spoke to him. Honest."

And the chance was gone.

# Chapter Eight

On Sunday morning the weather was cool and grey with rain threatening. Jon went out. He saw police cars parked in several streets on the estate and officers knocking on doors. So they were still asking questions; they could still catch him out. He stayed outside till lunchtime in case they called at his house again.

After lunch Mum made a pot of tea and switched on the television. "There's bound to be something about Ryan."

And there was: Tanya, making an appeal to anyone who might be holding Ryan against his will. Jon was taken aback by the change in her appearance: not only her face, but her whole personality seemed to have shrunk, collapsed inwards.

Steve sat beside her, his arm round her shoulders, while she whispered her tearful appeal and the cameras flashed and microphones bobbed in the foreground. The appeal ended with Tanya no longer able to speak and Steve, red-eyed, taking over, saying how much Ryan's sisters were missing him.

Jon was appalled. He thought of Tanya: big, happy-go-lucky Tanya, alternately laughing and yelling at the kids, dishing out crisps and chocolate bars, making him feel like one of the family. Tanya, reduced to this.

He looked at Mum. She was pink around the eyes.

The news report continued. The police wanted the man in the red car to come forward; they were searching the river and canals (Jon's hopes leapt); enquiries on the estate continued. There was film of the street, the underpass, the perimeter road where Ryan was supposed to have met the imaginary man...

When the weather news came on, promising more rain, Mum switched the TV off.

"I'm going to see Tanya," she said.

She was gone for half an hour. When she came back she had Paula and Lynette with her. Paula was clutching her favourite toy pony and Lynette had a doll.

Jon stared. "What are they doing here?"

"It seemed the least I could do," said Mum. "Tanya's under sedation and Steve's got his hands full with the baby and fending off the press. Go and find some toys, Jon. You've got Lego, haven't you, and those plastic animals?"

Jon went up to his room and delved under the bed, pushing aside his wet trainers to reach the Lego box. When he came back the little girls were running about laughing.

"Play with us, Jon," said Paula eagerly. "Be a monster."

"Like when you were a monster at our house," said Lynette, causing Mum to give Jon a surprised glance.

The last thing Jon wanted now was to play with Paula and Lynette. But he plunged into the game before they could give him away to Mum. He roared, and they squealed in delight and hid behind the settee.

"Hide! Hide! He's coming to find us!"

Later, when the floor was covered in Lego and the cushions were squashed and flung about, Mum fed them all baked beans on toast. Jon was helping her clear away the dirty dishes when the doorbell rang. It was Steve, come to fetch the girls. They ran to him, chattering.

"Thanks for having them, Gail," said Steve.

"That's all right. Anything I can do, just give me a ring. And try not to worry."

It didn't sound like Mum.

I wish she was always like this, Jon thought – friendly, joining in, like other people's mums.

Steve thanked her again, and said the girls would go to their nan's tomorrow, "if there's still no news". Jon heard the bleak hopelessness in Steve's voice, and thought, I've caused that.

Mum waved as the three of them went down the path. Then she shut the door, pushed back her hair, and sighed. "Those girls are a handful!" But she was bright-eyed, almost as if she'd enjoyed having her tidy house turned upside down.

The doorbell chimed again.

"Lynette's doll," said Mum.

The doll was on the hall table. She picked it up – and opened the door to the police.

# Chapter Nine

There were two of them this time: PC Norris and a woman, WPC Clarke. They wanted to speak to Jon.

"Come in," Mum said. "I'll make some tea."

But they said no; they thought it would be best if Jon and his mother came to the police station.

Jon said nothing; he was too scared. But Mum began gabbling breathlessly. "At the station? But he hasn't... He's told you... He doesn't know anything..."

And Jon knew then that she suspected him, but didn't want to believe it.

WPC Clarke reassured her. "Don't worry, Mrs Edey. It's just a formality. We need to check his statement – clear up a few things."

Jon was terrified. All he could think was: I must stick to my story. If I crack, they'll keep me there. They'll arrest me. I'll go to prison – or a ... what is it? ... a young offenders' institution. And Mum – how could I ever explain to her?

"You told us you saw Ryan Jackson talking to a man in a red Peugeot near Leeson Drive at eight-fifteen on Friday morning."

"Yes."

"Are you sure about that?"

"Yes."

"You don't want to change your statement?"

Jon couldn't see his mother, but he was aware of her, sitting somewhere behind him. "No," he whispered.

PC Norris leant back in his chair. "You see, Jonathan, we haven't been able to trace anyone else who witnessed this incident. No one else noticed the car, or the man. The man himself hasn't come forward."

"He – he probably only stopped for a moment. I mean, I never said he'd abducted Ryan. It's all on the telly but I never said it..."

"Nobody has said this man abducted Ryan," PC Norris agreed. "But you were well aware, when you told us about him, that we would consider that possibility."

"Yes." Jon could feel Mum's presence, tense and silent, behind him. She'd been asked not to intervene. But had she guessed he was lying? He looked up, defiant; how could anyone know? "But I did see him. And I thought I ought to tell you."

"Quite right. We also sent officers to the Summerlees estate" – Jon's heart began beating faster – "in the hope of tracking down a boy called Jason, a boy of about twelve, fair hair, five feet tall: a boy who looked a bit like Ryan.

We had no luck there, either."

"He might not live on Summerlees. I'm not sure. It might be Dorlands."

"Or it might be your imagination?"

He heard the scrape of a chair behind him as Mum got to her feet. "Are you calling my son a liar?"

"Please, Mrs Edey," said WPC Clarke.

"I didn't make it up," said Jon. He believed in Jason; he held on to him.

"Jonathan," said PC Norris, "we spoke to the manager of the fish and chip shop on the Summerlees estate. He remembers selling chips and Coke to two boys at around eleven-thirty on Friday morning. One of those boys he is sure was Ryan. The other boy was brown-haired, dressed in jeans and a black jumper with a leopard or tiger design on it."

Mum exclaimed, "Jonathan was in his school uniform on Friday. You *said* people recognized it!"

PC Norris ignored her. "Do you have a jumper like that, Jonathan?"

Jon thought of the damp clothes at the bottom of the laundry basket. "Yes, but—"

"Loads of kids have those jumpers!" said Mum.

"Mrs Edey—" WPC Clarke remonstrated again.

PC Norris continued, "These two boys were seen by a number of people: a woman walking her dog in the woods and another woman who chased off two boys throwing stones on the canal path. They all thought they recognized Ryan. But later in the day several children reported seeing a dishevelled boy running through the Eldon Wood estate at about half past four. This boy fits the description of the boy seen with Ryan earlier."

He jolted forward in the chair, abruptly. "What happened to Ryan, Jonathan?"

Mum drew in her breath, and Jon stared at the policeman, terrified. "I don't know. It wasn't me."

WPC Clarke intervened. Her voice was

reassuring. "If Ryan has had an accident, Jon, you must tell us. It doesn't matter if you were doing something you shouldn't have been."

Jon felt Mum's eyes on him. He wanted to tell the policewoman, but how could he? How could he do that to Mum? Admit that he'd played truant, stolen the boat, lied to the police. He couldn't tell now. It was too late. "I was at school," he insisted.

PC Norris sighed and leant back again.

"You know we can check that, Jonathan?"

Jon nodded. He was trapped. But he'd still play for time.

WPC Clarke said, "Jonathan, are you covering up for someone?"

And PC Norris said, "You do realize that if Ryan is outdoors, he could die?"

"I was at school," said Jon.

"What's going on?" Mum demanded. "Jonathan, what have you done?"

She had sat silent all the way home in the police car, but now she turned on him, and he could see that she was scared as well as angry.

He bolted for the stairs. "I need the loo."

He shot into the bathroom, pulled out the still-damp clothes and stuffed them to the back of the space under his bed. Back in the bathroom, he locked the door.

The window was open, and he heard, outside, the throb of rotor blades. He leaned out, and saw a police helicopter, white, with an orange stripe. So they were searching. They didn't believe the story about the red car. They'd be searching the woods and canal, where he and Ryan had been seen.

"Jonathan! I want to talk to you!"

He opened the door and went downstairs.

Mum was in the living-room, at the window.

The sound of the helicopter vibrated on the air, fading as it moved away.

She turned to him, accusing. "Jonathan, why do they keep coming back to you?"

"I don't know. It must be a mistake."

"But you were at school – weren't you?" she pleaded.

Jon wondered how long it would take them to find out: tomorrow morning at the latest. But they might know before – if they found his teacher, or the bus-driver.

"Yes!" he insisted. "It's stupid – people *saw* me in my uniform."

Mum latched on to this, eagerly. "Those jumpers – everyone was buying them. I'm going to complain about this, Jonathan: taking us in for questioning, accusing you of lying. They've no right!" She moved away from the window and trod on a piece of Lego. "We'd better get this lot tidied up."

They crawled around the floor, tossing pieces into the box.

"Mum," Jon began. He wanted to tell her. He wanted so much to tell her. But where to begin? She looked up, busy, trusting. "Mum,

I've ... got a tummy-ache." It was true. "I think I'll go to bed."

"All right." She looked concerned, and he knew she blamed the police. "You haven't been quite well all weekend, have you? Take the Lego up. Shall I bring you a drink?"

He shook his head.

Alone, in the bedroom, he heard the vacuum cleaner start up.

He lay thinking. The police interview replayed itself over and over in his head. He *did* feel ill. Sick, and shaky. But he couldn't sleep.

There was a television in his room. Just before ten he put the news on with the sound turned low. Ryan's face appeared, the familiar school photo. The bland voice of the newscaster told him that the police now believed that Ryan might have been the victim of an accident. A search of the local area had begun. Another boy was being sought...

Me, thought Jon. Me; they're hunting me.

A boy Ryan knew; a boy who wasn't at school on Friday.

Tomorrow, first thing, they'd check with the Thomas Crawford School – and then they'd be back here: "Where were you? Where *did* you go?"

And he would run out of lies.

Jon woke – and remembered.

He looked at the clock: 4 a.m. It was still dark. He'd only been asleep for an hour or so.

He got up and opened the curtains. The garden, the estate, the fields and woods beyond lay still and silent. The darkness was not the total black of midnight; it had a grey softness, and he knew that dawn was near. The moon was pale above the trees.

Out there, under that moon, was Ryan.

Jon turned away from the window and began dressing, quickly, clumsily, tugging the jumper over his head, struggling with inside-out sleeves.

In a few hours' time the police would know he had been lying. They would come for him. He didn't want to be here.

# Chapter Ten

Nothing moved on the estate. Curtains were drawn, gates closed. Jon's trainers – still damp from Friday – made scarcely a sound as he ran down the road towards the underpass, but his breath was loud and frightened: it seemed to fill the world.

He was across the main road and running towards the woods before he realized where his feet were taking him.

He hadn't thought about where to go – only that he must get away. But now he saw that there was only one place he *could* go.

Dew on the grass soaked his shoes once more

as he ran across the fields. The sky was lighter now, pearl-grey, and when he entered the woods he heard a bird begin to sing. Within minutes the trees were full of song. It was day. The day he couldn't escape from, no matter how far he ran.

Another familiar sound throbbed overhead: the helicopter. So early! They must be sure that Ryan wasn't far from home.

Sunlight glinted between the leaves. The dew sparkled. It was going to be a fine day, but the air was still cold.

Cold. Huddled on a ledge for three days and nights in rain and cold.

Was it a body they were looking for?

For the first time Jon thought about Ryan – really thought about what Ryan must have suffered. The hunger, the pain, the cold, the fear. When did Ryan realize that no one was coming? Did he guess what Jon had done – or not done? He'd hurt his arm – perhaps broken it. Was he in pain? Unconscious?

If he was conscious, he'd have heard the helicopter. He'd try to signal, old Ryan; he'd struggle, the way he'd struggled up to that ledge. He wasn't one to give up. But after three days, anyone would despair. Ryan must have thought he was going to die. And if he had...

All I cared about was me, thought Jon. Me getting into trouble. Me being found out. I never thought about what it must have been like to be abandoned on that ledge. And now – it could be too late.

He saw the road ahead of him, through the trees, and ran faster.

He recognized the place at once, even before he saw the sock he'd left in the cleft of the tree.

He stood at the top of the cliff and called, "Ryan!"

No answer.

He began to climb down.

The soil was loose from the recent rain, and he had to search for bushes strong enough to hold him. The overhang was the worst. When he was past that, with the rock curving above him, he called again, "Ryan!"

The silence was terrifying. He thought, Ryan's dead, dead. I'm going to find a dead body.

He couldn't look down beyond the next foothold. All his effort went into the climb. Every time he stopped he called again, but there was no sound, only bird song and the distant rush of water.

"Ryan!"

Below him now he saw the ledge. No sign of Ryan. But it curved round a bit, he remembered. Cautiously he lowered himself and landed on it.

Ryan wasn't there.

He took a deep breath.

And then he saw something. Further along the ledge a piece of blue denim was sticking out from a cleft in the rock.

He crept towards it. His heart was banging.

Ryan *was* there. The cleft was the entrance to a narrow cave that went back almost parallel to the ledge. Ryan must have crawled inside for shelter. It was just long enough for him – but too narrow for Jon to crawl in beside him. He knelt and put a hand on Ryan's ankle. It was cold.

"Ryan, are you alive? Ryan?"

Ryan moved, and murmured.

Relief brought a rush of tears to Jon's eyes. "I'm sorry. I'm so sorry."

He squeezed further in. Ryan's eyes flickered open. His face was very pale, and he muttered in a confused way. Jon took off his own jumper and wrapped it round him, being careful not to move the injured arm, which was still in its home-made sling.

"I'll get help," he said. "I will this time."

At that moment he heard the helicopter.

The sound of the rotor was overhead. He crawled out and stood up on the ledge. Through the leaves he could see it, moving upriver. He waved his arms, shouted.

The helicopter moved on.

"Don't go!" Jon shouted.

Now he experienced something of Ryan's despair. The tree cover on the cliff was too thick; they couldn't see him. He clambered down the cliff, slipping and gasping in his eagerness not to lose the helicopter. But by the time he reached the shore it had disappeared.

He ran back and forth along the tiny beach. There was no one on the river, no one to see him. And Ryan was so cold; he could die. In desperation Jon began climbing up again.

And then he heard it: a faint throbbing. He scrambled down. The helicopter was coming back: he saw the light flashing, and the orange stripe bright against the clouds. He jumped up and down and waved his arms and pointed to the cliff. "Help!" he shouted. "Help!" The helicopter came right overhead; its throbbing roar filled his mind.

He saw a man with a loud-hailer at the window. "Where is he?" the man shouted.

"On a ledge! Up there! His arm's broken."

"Right. We'll get someone to you. Don't try to climb. Wait there."

# Chapter Eleven

Jon opened his eyes, saw his mother sitting by the bed, and shut them again.

He didn't want to be awake. He couldn't take any more. The police telling-off had been bad enough. He'd felt so ashamed as they told him what a terrible thing he'd done, how he'd wasted their time and almost killed Ryan.

But facing Mum had been worse. She was in a state anyway, after finding his bed empty at 7 a.m. and then being told by the police that they were bringing him home. But it wasn't the fury and shouting that had upset him, it was the way she suddenly crumpled and just sat and cried. Over and over she said, "I can't believe you'd do a thing like that. I can't believe it." He knew he had utterly failed her.

At last she'd said, "You can't go to school today. You look terrible. Go to bed. I'll phone."

He lay still, now, feeling bruises and strained muscles from his climb and rescue. He remembered Ryan going up ahead of him, wrapped in blankets, his face so white; and PC Norris, back at the station, saying, "He's not out of danger yet, you know. He could still die."

Jon looked at his bedside clock. Six o'clock. He'd slept all day. And Ryan...?

He turned to his mother. "Ryan?" It came out as a croak.

"He's fine. He'll be in hospital for a few days, though." She was pale, tired-looking and without make-up. He realized she must have taken the day off work. "I brought you some juice and biscuits."

"Thanks." He sat up. The cool orange juice eased his throat.

"I rang the school," said Mum. "Said you were ill. I wasn't going to say anything about all this, but Mr Hammond rang back at lunchtime. We had a long talk. He thinks you're under too much stress. He wants to move you to a lower class."

"I know," he said. "But I – I was afraid to tell you."

Mum was fiddling with her rings, twisting them round her finger. "I never realized ... I mean, I just wanted the best for you, Jonathan. I wanted you to do well ... I didn't realize I was putting so much pressure on you. I mean, it's not *that* important, is it, school?" She looked up, managed a smile. "There's a parents' evening next week and we're going to talk about it some more. You too. Jonathan: you are happy there, aren't you, apart from the work?"

Jon didn't reply. He didn't want to talk about that – not to Mum. He might talk to Dad if he got the chance.

"Do they know what I did?" he asked. "The school?"

"No. Just that you played truant."

"Will it be in the papers?"

"The police said you won't be named. But everyone round here will know." Her voice cracked.

We could move, he thought, panicking. But that wasn't what he wanted – not really. He couldn't just run away. Not again.

"Does Tanya know?"

"Yes. I went to see her. To try to apologize."

"What happened?"

Mum looked down. "She called me a stuck-up little bitch and yelled at me to get out of her house. Steve had to calm her down. She said you were – well, you can imagine what she said. You know what Tanya's like when she's angry."

Jon did. But he wanted her to forgive him. He'd go round, later. He'd have to, even if she threw him out.

"I told her," Mum went on. "I told her it wasn't just you. It was Ryan who led you into it."

"No!" exclaimed Jon. "No, he didn't. I mean, it was his idea, but I didn't have to go along with it. I knew it was wrong to take the boat. I knew I should have gone to school. It was just as much my fault."

"Well. Steve says to give her time. He's OK, is Steve. I've said some things about him, but he's not a bad sort." She picked up the glass and the empty plate. "But that Ryan: he's a bad influence."

"Mum, he's not!" Jon was shouting now. "It was me – *my* fault. Ryan's never done anything as bad as what I did. He would never have left *me* on that ledge."

He got up, and began dressing. "Will you take me to the hospital?'

"Now?"

"I've got to see Ryan."

*   *   *

Mum found herself a seat outside the ward. "I'll wait here."

Jon faced her, and took a breath. "Mum, I've been friends with Ryan for ages. I go round to his house after school."

"I'd begun to realize that."

"I'm going to stay friends with him, if – if he still wants me to."

"Right."

But he could see she didn't like it.

He moved towards the ward entrance.

"Jonathan?" She looked unsure of herself – even a bit guilty. "Your dad phoned again while you were asleep – about Whitsun. I was putting him off ... you know..."

Jon knew.

"But perhaps you should go. Get away for a bit. Think about what you've done. And you can talk to your dad..."

"Yes," said Jon, and his spirits lifted, just a little. "Yes. I will. I'll go."

But first there was Ryan.

He pushed open the heavy doors to the ward and went inside.